Hank and Fred
Fred and Hank

HANK and FRED
FRED and HANK

by Wendy Kindred

J. B. Lippincott Company
Philadelphia and New York

U.S. Library of Congress Cataloging in Pub-
lication Data. Kindred, Wendy. Hank and
Fred. SUMMARY: The adventures of two
young boys discovering each other's friend-
ship. [1. Friendship-Fiction] I. Title. PZ7.K567-
Han [E]   75-35518   ISBN-0-397-31672-0

One morning in the summer in the hot and smelly city, Hank went out looking for a friend.

He looked
low and high
until he found
one. Then. . .

Hank and Fred played

together all that day...

and all the next day

too . . .

and

many days thereafter.

But one day as Hank was going to meet Fred, he met some other kids.

"I'm going to meet my new friend, Fred," he said. "Wanna come?"

They waited for Fred.
He didn't come.
They waited...

and waited . . .

but Fred didn't come.

So they left.

Then Fred came.

Fred and Hank played

together

all that day...

and many days
thereafter.

WENDY KINDRED is a teacher, artist, and writer. She holds a master of fine arts degree from the University of Chicago and has lived in many places, including Vienna, Austria; Grenoble, France; and Addis Ababa, Ethiopia. The author of four books of fiction for young readers, she now lives with her twin daughters in Fort Kent, Maine, where she is an assistant professor of art at the University of Maine. For recreation, she likes to ski, hike through the woods and potato fields, and go camping.

DATE DUE
